MOODY
MARGARET'S
Makeover

MOODY MARGARET'S Makeover

Francesca Simon

Illustrated by Tony Ross

Orion
Children's Books

Moody Margaret's Makeover originally appeared in
Horrid Henry and the Abominable Snowman
first published in Great Britain in 2007 by Orion Children's Books
This edition first published in Great Britain in 2013
by Orion Children's Books
a division of the Orion Publishing Group Ltd
Orion House
5 Upper Saint Martin's Lane
London WC2H 9EA
An Hachette UK Company

1 3 5 7 9 10 8 6 4 2

The Orion Publishing Group's policy is to use papers that
are natural, renewable and recyclable products and made
from wood grown in sustainable forests. The logging and
manufacturing processes are expected to conform to the
environmental regulations of the country of origin.

A catalogue record for this book is available from the British Library.

ISBN 978 1 4440 0119 8
Printed in China

www.orionbooks.co.uk
www.horridhenry.co.uk

There are many more **Horrid Henry** books available.
For a complete list visit
www.horridhenry.co.uk
or
www.orionbooks.co.uk

Contents

Chapter 1

"Watch out, Gurinder!
You're smearing your nail varnish,"
screeched Moody Margaret.
"Violet! Don't touch your face –
you're spoiling all my hard work.
Susan! Sit still."

"I am sitting still," said Sour Susan. "Stop pulling my hair."

"I'm not pulling your hair," hissed Margaret. "I'm styling it."

"Ouch!" squealed Susan. "You're hurting me."

"I am not, crybaby."

"I'm not a crybaby," howled Susan.

Moody Margaret sighed loudly.
"Not everyone can be naturally
beautiful like me. Some people" –
she glared at Susan –
"have to work at it."

"You're not beautiful,"
said Sour Susan, snorting.

"I am too," said Margaret,
preening herself.

"Are not," said Susan.
"On the ugly scale of 1 to 10,
with 1 being the ugliest,
wartiest toad, you're a 2."

"Huh!" said Margaret.
"Well, you're so ugly you're
minus 1. They don't have an ugly
enough scale for you."

"I want my
money back!"
shrieked Susan.

"No way!"
shrieked Margaret.
"Now sit down
and shut up."

Across the wall in the next garden,
deep inside the branches hiding
the top secret entrance of the
Purple Hand fort, a master spy
pricked up his ears.

Money?
Had he heard the word *money*?
What was going on next door?

Horrid Henry zipped out of his fort
and dashed to the low wall separating
his garden from Margaret's.
Then he stared.
And stared some more.

He'd seen many weird things in
his life. But nothing as weird as this.

Chapter 2

Moody Margaret, Sour Susan,
Lazy Linda, Vain Violet and
Gorgeous Gurinder were sitting
in Margaret's garden.

Susan had rollers tangling her pink hair. Violet had blue mascara all over her face. Linda was covered in gold glitter. There was spilt nail varnish, face powder, and broken lipstick all over Margaret's patio.

Horrid Henry burst out laughing.
"Are you playing clowns?"
said Henry.

"Huh, that's how much you know,
Henry," said Margaret.
"I'm doing makeovers."

"What's that?" said Henry.

"It's when you change how people look, dummy," said Margaret.

"I knew that," lied Henry. "I just wanted to see if you did."

Margaret waved a leaflet in his face.

Makeovers? *Makeovers?*
What an incredibly stupid idea.
Who'd pay to have a moody old
grouch like Margaret smear gunk all
over their face? Ha! No one.
Horrid Henry started laughing
and pointing.

Vain Violet looked like a demon
with red and blue and purple gloop
all over her face.

Gorgeous
Gurinder looked
as if a paint pot
had been poured
down her cheeks.

Linda's hair
looked as if
she'd been
struck by
lightning.

But Violet wasn't screaming and yanking Margaret's hair out. Instead she handed Margaret – money.

"Thanks, Margaret, I look amazing," said Vain Violet, admiring herself in the mirror.

Henry waited for the mirror to crack. It didn't.

"Thanks, Margaret," said Gurinder.
"I look so fantastic
I hardly recognise myself." And she
also handed Margaret a pound.
Two whole pounds?
Were they mad?

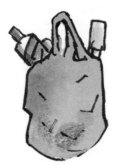

Chapter 3

"Are you getting ready for the Monster's Ball?" jeered Henry.

"Shut up, Henry," said Vain Violet.

"Shut up, Henry,"
said Gorgeous Gurinder.

"You're just jealous because I'm going to be rich and you're not," said Margaret.
"Nah nah ne nah nah."

"Why don't we give Henry a makeover?" said Violet.

"Good idea," said Moody Margaret. "He could sure use one."

"Yeah," said Sour Susan.

Horrid Henry took a step back.

Margaret advanced towards him
wielding nail varnish and a hairbrush.
Violet followed clutching a lipstick,
spray dye and other instruments
of torture.

Yikes! Horrid Henry nipped back
to the safety of his fort as fast as
he could, trying to ignore the
horrible, cackling laughter.

He sat on his Purple Hand throne and scoffed some extra tasty chocolate biscuits from the secret stash he'd nicked from Margaret yesterday.

Makeovers! Ha! How dumb could you get? Trust a pea-brained grouch like Margaret to come up with such a stupid idea. Who in their right mind would want a makeover?

On the other hand…
Horrid Henry had actually seen
Margaret being paid. And good
money too, just for smearing some
coloured gunk onto people's faces
and yanking their hair about.

Hmmmn. Horrid Henry started to think. Maybe Margaret *did* have a little eensy-weensy teeny-tiny bit of a good idea. And, naturally, anything she could do, Henry could do much, much better.

Margaret obviously didn't know
the first thing about makeovers, so
why should *she* make all that money,
thought Horrid Henry indignantly.
He'd steal – no, *borrow* – her idea
and do it better.
Much much better. He'd make
people look *really* fantastic.

Henry's Makeovers.
Henry's Marvellous Makeovers.
Henry's Miraculous Makeovers.
He'd be rich!

Chapter 4

With some false teeth and red marker he could turn Miss Battle-Axe into a vampire.

Mrs Oddbod could be a perfect
Dracula.

And wouldn't Stuck-Up Steve
be improved after a short visit from
the Makeover Magician?

Even Aunt Ruby wouldn't recognise
him when Henry had finished.
Tee hee.

First, he needed supplies.
That was easy: Mum had tons of
gunk for smearing all over her face.
And if he ran out he could always
use crayons and glue.

Horrid Henry dashed to the
bathroom and helped himself to
a few handfuls of Mum's makeup.
What on earth did she need all this
stuff for, thought Henry, piling it
into a bag. About time someone
cleared out this drawer.

Then he wrote a few leaflets.

Horrid Henry, Makeover Magician,
was ready for business.

All he needed were some customers.
Preferably rich, ugly customers.
Now, where could he find some
of those?

Henry strolled into the sitting room.
Dad was reading on the sofa. Mum
was working at the computer.
Horrid Henry looked at his aged,
wrinkly, boring old parents.
Blecccch!

Boy, could they be improved,
thought Henry.
How could he tactfully persuade
these potential customers that they
needed his help – fast?

"Mum," said Henry.
"You know Great-Aunt Greta?"

"Yes," said Mum.

"Well, you're starting
to look just like her."

"*What*?" said Mum.

"Yup," said Horrid Henry.
"Old and ugly. Except…" He peered
at her. "You have more wrinkles."

"*What?*" squeaked Mum.

47

"And Dad looks like a gargoyle,"
said Henry.

"Huh?" said Dad.

"Only scarier," said Henry.
"But don't worry, I can help."

"Oh really?" said Mum.

"Oh really?" said Dad.

"Yeah," said Henry.
"I'm doing makeovers."

He handed Mum and Dad a leaflet.

Are you Ugly?
Are you Very Very ugly?
Do you look like the creature
from the Black Lagoon?
(Only WORSE?)
Then today is your luckyday!

HENRY'S
MARVELLOUS
MAKEOVERS

Only £2 for an exciting new you!!!

"So, how many makeovers would you like?" said Horrid Henry. "Ten? Twenty? Maybe more 'cause you're so old and need a lot of work to fix you."

"Make over someone else,"
said Mum, scowling.

"Make over someone else,"
said Dad, scowling.

Boy, talk about ungrateful,
thought Horrid Henry.

Chapter 5

"Me first!"

"No, me!"

Screams were coming from
Margaret's garden.

Kung-Fu Kate and Singing Soraya
were about to become her latest
victims.

Well, not if Henry could help it.

"Step right up, get your makeovers here!" shouted Henry. "Miracle Makeovers, from an expert. Only £2 for a brand new you."

"Leave my customers alone,
copycat!" hissed Moody Margaret,
holding out her hand to snatch
Kate's pound.
Henry ignored her.

"You look boring, Kate,"
said Henry. "Why don't you let a
real expert give you a makeover?"

"You?" said Kate.

"Two pounds and you'll look
completely different,"
said Horrid Henry. "Guaranteed."

"Margaret's only charging £1,"
said Kate.

"My special offer today is 75p for the
first makeover," said Henry quickly.
"And free beauty advice," he added.

Soraya looked up. Kate stood up
from Margaret's chair.

"Such as?" scowled Margaret.
"Go on, tell us."

Eeeek.

What on earth was a beauty tip?
If your face is dirty, wash it?
Use a nit comb?
Horrid Henry had no idea.

"Well, in your case wear a bag
over your head," said Horrid Henry.
"Or a bucket."

Susan snickered.

"Ha ha, very funny,"
snapped Margaret.
"Come on, Kate. Don't let him trick
you. I'm the makeover expert."

"I'm going to try Henry," said Kate.

"Me too," said Soraya.

Yippee! His first customers.
Henry stuck out his tongue
at Margaret.

Kung-Fu Kate and Singing Soraya
climbed over the wall and sat down
on the bench at the picnic table.
Henry opened his makeover bag
and got to work.

"No peeking," said Henry.
"I want you to be surprised."

Chapter 6

Henry smeared and coated, primped and coloured, slopped and glopped. This was easy!

"I'm so beautiful – hoo hoo hoo,"
hummed Soraya.

"Aren't you going to do my hair?"
said Kung-Fu Kate.

"Naturally," said Horrid Henry.
He emptied a pot of glue on her
head and scrunched it around.

"What have you put in?" said Kate.

"Secret hair potion," said Henry.

"What about *me*?" said Soraya.

"No problem," said Henry, shovelling in some red paint. A bit of black here, a few blobs of red there, a smear of purple and … way hey!

Henry stood back to admire his handiwork. Wow! Kung-Fu Kate looked *completely* different. So did Singing Soraya. Next time he'd charge £10. The moment people saw them everyone would want one of Henry's marvellous makeovers.

"You look amazing,"
said Horrid Henry.
He had no idea he was such
a brilliant makeover artist.
Customers would be queuing
for his services.
He'd need a bigger piggybank.

"There, just like the Mummy, Frankenstein, and a vampire," said Henry, handing Kate a mirror.

"AAAARRRRGGGGGHHH!"

screamed Kung-Fu Kate.

Soraya snatched the mirror.

"AAAARRRRGGGGGHHH!"

screamed Singing Soraya.

Horrid Henry stared at them.
Honestly, there was no pleasing
some people.

"NOOOOOOOOO!" squealed
Kung-Fu Kate.

"But I thought you wanted to
look amazing," said Henry.

"Amazingly good! Not scary!"
wailed Kate.

"Has anyone seen my new lipsticks?" said Mum. "I could have sworn I put them in the…"

She caught sight of Soraya and Kate.

"AAAARRRRGGGGGHHH!" screeched Mum. "Henry! How could you be so horrid? Go to your room."

"But ... but..." gasped Horrid
Henry. It was so unfair. Was it his
fault his stupid customers didn't
know when they looked great?
Henry stomped up the stairs.
Then he sighed. Maybe he did need
a little more makeover practice
before he opened for business.
Now, where could he find someone
to practise on?

"I got an A on my spelling test,"
said Perfect Peter.

"I got a gold star for having the
tidiest drawer," said Tidy Ted.

"And I got in the Good as Gold
book again," said Goody-Goody
Gordon.

Henry burst into Peter's bedroom.

"I'm doing makeovers," said Horrid Henry. "Who wants to go first?"

"Uhhmmm," said Peter.

"Uhhmmm," said Ted.

"We're going to Sam's birthday party today," said Gordon.

"Even better," said Henry, beaming.
"I can make you look great for the
party. Who's first?"

What are you going to read next?

More adventures with Horrid Henry,

or go to sea with Poppy the Pirate Dog,

or into space with Cudweed.

You could have fun on A Rainbow Shopping Day,

or explore Down in the Jungle,

but watch out for

A Creepy Crawly Story!

Make magic with

The Three Little Witches,

and have
a ball
with

Princesses.

Or follow the star in

The First Christmas.

Enjoy all the Early Readers.